5 Minute Storytime

Children who are read to are inspired to read, so cuddle up for a **5 MINUTE STORYTIME** and expand your child's mind as you build a lifelong   for reading and learning.

We cannot, however, guarantee your 5 minute break won't turn into 10, 15, or 30 minutes, as these **FUN** stories and engaging pictures will have you turning the pages **AGAIN** and **AGAIN**!

Designed by Flowerpot Press
in Franklin, TN.
www.FlowerpotPress.com
Designer: Mickenzie Smith
Editor: Katrine Crow
ROR-0811-0122
ISBN: 978-1-4867-1276-2
Made in China/Fabriqué en Chine

Chicken
Little

A CAUTIONARY TALE

RETOLD BY
GEORGE BRIDGE

ILLUSTRATED BY
BEA MORITZ

One day, a few years ago,
Chicken Little caused quite a panic.

This is what happened...

Chicken Little was leaving for school on a sunny, happy morning, when an acorn fell from a tree and landed on his head.

PANIC!

Chicken Little got scared.

Henny Penny was walking to
school when she heard the news.

PANIC!
She was really scared,
so she ran with her friend.

Turkey Lurkey was waiting for the school bus
when he heard the news.

PANIC!
He was really scared,
so he ran with his friends.

"The sky is falling!!!"
"The sky is falling!!!"

Chicken Little, and Henny Penny, and
Turkey Lurkey screamed as they ran.

Dizzy Ducky was skateboarding to
school when she heard the news.

PANIC!
She was really scared,
so she ran with her friends.

"The sky is falling!!!"
"The sky is falling!!!"

Chicken Little, and Henny Penny,
and Turkey Lurkey, and Dizzy Ducky
screamed as they ran.

Foxy Loxy was sitting outside his cave feeling hungry when he heard the news.

OPPORTUNITY!

He wasn't scared, but he was hungry.
"RUN IN HERE!!! RUN IN HERE!!!"
he screamed, and that is just what the
friends did.
"NOW I'VE GOT YOU! FEED ME!"
shouted Foxy Loxy as he
slammed the door.

Stuck inside the cave, the friends began to think. Then they began to talk. Then they began to figure out what had started the panic. Then they felt silly.

"We need to get out of here,"
said, Chicken Little.
Now, instead of being scared,
Chicken Little felt brave.
All of his friends
followed Chicken Little
as he snuck out of
the cave and into
the sunshine.

Then they ran off
to school.

"Life is good!"

Chicken Little, and Henny Penny,
and Turkey Lurkey, and Dizzy Ducky
screamed as they ran.

And from that day forward, Chicken Little, and Henny Penny, and Turkey Lurkey, and Dizzy Ducky did not get scared so easily.

They did not panic. They knew that being brave and staying cool was way more fun!

The End.